Not A Used Dog, At All

This is my book.
My name is

Nuala Egan

My favorite dog names

_____

_____

_____

AuthorHouse™
1663 Liberty Drive
Bloomington, IN 47403
www.authorhouse.com
Phone: 1-800-839-8640

First published by AuthorHouse 9/3/2009

ISBN: 978-1-4389-5204-8 (sc)

Library of Congress Control Number: 2009905182

Printed in the United States of America
Bloomington, Indiana

This book is printed on acid-free paper.

authorHOUSE®

Not A Used Dog, At All

by Carol Erickson
Illustrations by Jeff McCloskey

Dedicated:
To everyone who has loved a dog.

Carol Erickson

Dedicated:
To my Wife Lori.

Jeff McCloskey

FOOT-STOMPING, ARMS-CROSSED, SQUINTY-EYED MAD! Matt stormed around his bedroom, looking wild as the dinosaurs on his blanket.

"No shelter dog, Mommy," he said. "I'm serious."

"No pet store puppy, Matt," his mom said. "I'm serious."

No! No! No! hung all over the room.

1

Matt didn't like "NO!", unless he was the one saying it. He frowned.
His mouth turned down. He wouldn't smile. He wouldn't listen. Most of all...

He wouldn't stop talking.

"Animal shelters are noisy," Matt said, covering his ears. "And smelly." He pinched his nose so tight he sounded weird. "Shelters have used dogs that belonged to somebody else. I only want to buy a brand new puppy from the pet store at the mall. I'm serious."

By now, Matt's mom had seen enough of his crazy faces. She knew what she had to do. She opened the squeaky kitchen drawer, pulled out a knife and...

Cut a heart shaped peanut butter sandwich to put on his special dinosaur plate. It was lunchtime, and maybe Matt would listen while he ate.

"Some shelter dogs did have owners who gave them away," his mom said, "but these dogs still want to be part of loving families. Families like ours."

Matt slowly chewed his sandwich, thinking about used shelter dogs, new pet store puppies, and a tooth that suddenly wobbled so much in all that sticky peanut butter that...

He could wiggle it almost in a circle with his tongue as he sat in the car after lunch. He hoped this loose tooth meant good luck and a trip to the pet store.

NOT.

Matt's mom drove right past the mall and headed straight to that smelly shelter where just then...

Walking in front of the shelter, a scarf wearing dog and a family. They sure looked familiar.

"Mommy, I think that's...," Matt was so excited he couldn't get the words out.

"Might be," his mom said, waving at them. "Even President's families should adopt from shelters and rescues."

Matt jumped out of the car, but the family and the dog had gotten into a limousine and driven away. Now he was stuck going into the noisy shelter, where the dogs might even have missing hair like...

Bald Mr. Coleman, the animal shelter manager, who sat at his desk finishing a peanut butter sandwich. He had a big space between his front teeth and an even bigger smile.

"What kind of dog are you looking for? Big dog? Little dog? Fast dog? Slow dog? Furry dog? Slick dog? Quiet dog? Noisy dog? Sitting dog? Jumping dog? We have them all. And oh, by the way, all the dogs have more hair than I do!"

Mr. Coleman rubbed his smooth head but...

Matt just shook his. "I want a BRAND NEW puppy. With soft feet. Soft fur. Bought at the pet store at the mall. Not a used dog, at all."

"Not a used dog, at all. Hmm. Let's go to the 'not a used dog' section. We have a lot of dogs there." He led them right to...

Big dogs and little dogs in cages lined up along the walls.

Some barked.

Some jumped.

Some wagged.

One...

WIGGLES
Needs A Home

Dog looked right at Matt.

"What do you think of him?" Mr. Coleman asked. "Black dogs have a hard time getting adopted because they aren't fancy looking. But Wiggles is smart, friendly, and needs a brand new kid of his own to play with. Why, he'd even take a used kid!"

Matt didn't laugh. He circled his loose tooth with his tongue and studied the black dog in the cage. Wiggles wasn't fluffy. He wasn't pretty. His grey mustache showed he was just an old dog, not a cute young puppy like Matt wanted.

Matt turned away from the cage. He was ready to leave.

But Wiggles wasn't through with Matt. He barked one time, stuck a spongy black nose and pink tongue through the cage bars, and wagged his long tail back and forth. Matt took a second look.

He petted Wiggles in the cage and talked softly to him for a long time. He had wanted a new pet store puppy. But what about this used shelter dog? Puppy? Shelter dog? Matt's mind went back and forth, just like Wiggles' tail. Finally, he decided.

"Mommy," he said, "I still want to go to the pet store. I'm serious."

His mother looked at the friendly black dog. "But what about Wiggles?" she asked.

Matt shook his head. "It's not good enough."

"What's not good enough?" his mom asked.

"Having him sleep on the floor," Matt said. "He's so nice and beautiful, he needs a new bed of his own and some toys from a pet store! I want him to come home with us!!"

Mr. Coleman and Matt had matching smiles. "I knew you were a smart kid the minute you walked in. Wiggles will be your best friend. Buy his toys and bed from a pet store but don't buy pet store puppies. Your mom knows why."

Matt looked at his mother. "What does he mean?"

"Pet store puppies usually come from very bad places called puppy mills. The dogs live in terrible conditions," she explained. "If people keep buying pet store puppies, pet stores will want even more puppies to be born in these puppy mills. Adopting from a shelter like we are helps shut down cruel puppy mills AND saves a grown up dog's life."

Matt thought about it, and at the instant he understood, his very loose tooth broke free. It fell with a *ping* in the center of feet and paws.

"Looks like you lost a used tooth and the idea of a pet store puppy. Matt, sometimes things work out better when we don't get what we first want," Mr. Coleman said. "Go ahead, unlock Wiggles' cage."

Matt carefully lifted the latch. The door creaked open.

Wiggles' eyes brightened. Right then, something magical happened, like it does at adoption time in every shelter.

When Wiggles and Matt hugged, the old black dog suddenly transformed into a BRAND NEW DOG, Not A Used Dog, At All. Matt changed, too.

"Mommy, I saved his life! Wait till I tell everybody!"

"Yes, you made a difference in the world, starting with this dog. Way to go, Matt," she said.

The new family rode home together, Wiggles' tail happily thumping against the backseat.

"Mommy, Wiggles is the greatest dog ever, and he's the nicest shade of black I've ever seen. I'm serious!" Matt couldn't stop grinning and showing off the new space in his smile.

That night, Matt's mother peeked in his room. All the **No's** from that morning had vanished. Even the bedroom dinosaurs with their big teeth looked happy. Speaking of teeth, what had Matt done with his tooth?

She smoothed his pillow and felt something underneath. It was a heart shaped note with a little white tooth taped to it.

Thank you for my new dog! Love, Matt.

Where was that new dog? Matt's mom looked all around. She couldn't see him...

WIGGLES

But she heard him. Snuggled in his own new bed near Matt, Wiggles snored loudly. Matt's mom smiled.

And for the first time that dog-adopting, tooth-losing day, Matt was finally quiet. That made her smile even bigger.

23

NOTE TO PARENTS AND TEACHERS

BLACK DOGS

Big, black dogs are the least likely to be adopted from shelters in the United States, according to many shelter managers. The exact reason for that is unclear, but many adoptable, loving dogs are euthanized simply because of their color and size.

PUPPY MILLS

According to the PSPCA, puppy mills are factory farms where dogs are bred in unsafe, unsanitary and inhumane conditions. Puppy mill dogs are:

• Kept in cages far too small

• Deprived of proper nutrition, veterinary care and socialization.

The retail outlets for these puppies are pet stores and internet sites. To help in the fight against puppy mills, the Pennsylvania SPCA encourages people not to purchase animals from these locations. Not buying puppies or supplies from any pet store or internet site that sells puppies will help end puppy mills and the resulting shelter overcrowding.

As Pennsylvania's leading humane law enforcement unit, the PSPCA responds to complaints and conducts undercover investigations. Adopting from and donating to shelters can help make life better for so many animals.

For more information, visit www.PSPCA.org

Carol Erickson, an Emmy winning news reporter for KYW-TV in Philadelphia, Pennsylvania, is well known for promoting pet adoption and responsible care of animals in her TV reports. She has hosted the station's "Ask the Vet" segment for more than a decade. In her role as a Certified Broadcast Meteorologist, Carol can be counted on to remind viewers to protect their pets during extreme weather conditions. She earned a diploma in Canine Behavior Counseling because of her interest in how dogs think after observing her shelter dog Riley.

The recipient of the Pennsylvania SPCA's Media All Star Award, Carol has a grown daughter and shares her life on a New Jersey farm with dogs and horses.

Author's profits from this book will be donated to animal shelters and rescue groups.

Jeff McCloskey an Emmy winning graphic designer and graduate of the Art Institute of Philadelphia, has been designing and animating graphics for television since 1986. This is the first time he has illustrated a children's book. Jeff currently works and lives in Philadelphia with his wife Lori and their 2 dogs and 4 cats.

LaVergne, TN USA
01 November 2009
162644LV00002B

9781438952048